SPACE
UNIVERSITY™

THE SPACE
EXPLORER'S
GUIDE TO

Life Aboard the International Space Station

BY
HENA KHAN

WITH
RACHEL CONNOLLY
SPACE EDUCATOR

MINNA PALAQUIBAY
SPACE EDUCATOR

RYAN WYATT
VISUAL ADVISOR

AND
JIM SWEITZER, PH.D.
NASA SCIENCE CENTER,
DePAUL UNIVERSITY

SCHOLASTIC INC.

NEW YORK   TORONTO   LONDON   AUCKLAND   SYDNEY
MEXICO CITY   NEW DELHI   HONG KONG   BUENOS AIRES

Who's Who at Space U

Hena Khan
Writer

Hena is a writer who's stationed on Earth—at least for now! She lives in Maryland with her husband and son, where she enjoys writing books for Space University.

Rachel Connolly
Consultant

Rachel manages the astrophysics education program at the American Museum of Natural History's Rose Center for Earth and Space.

Ryan Wyatt
Visual Advisor

Ryan designs scientific visuals for the American Museum of Natural History's Rose Center for Earth and Space.

Minna Palaquibay
Consultant

Minna designs and teaches science programs for kids at the American Museum of Natural History's Rose Center for Earth and Space.

Jim Sweitzer
Advisor

Jim is an astrophysicist and the director of the NASA Space Science Center at DePaul University in Chicago.

With special thanks to:

Mike Gentry, Paula Vargas, Curt Peternell, and Ken Bowersox at NASA's Johnson Space Center. Also thanks to Marianne Dyson.

ISBN: 0-439-55744-5
Copyright © 2004 by Scholastic Inc.

Editor: Andrea Menotti
Assistant Editor: Megan Gendell
Designers: Peggy Gardner, Lee Kaplan, Tricia Kleinot
Illustrators: Daniel Aycock, Yancey C. Labat, Ed Shems

Photos: All images provided by NASA unless otherwise noted below.
Front cover: The International Space Station, photographed from below by an astronaut onboard the space shuttle *Atlantis*
Back cover: The International Space Station over the Earth, photographed from the space shuttle *Atlantis*
Title page: Another image of the International Space Station, taken from the space shuttle *Endeavor*
Page 44 (*Soyuz* landing): NASA/Marty Linde.

12 11 10 9 8 7 6 5 4 3 2 1   4 5 6 7 8 9/0

Printed in the U.S.A.

First Scholastic printing, March 2004

The publisher has made every effort to ensure that the activities in this book are safe when done as instructed. Adults should provide guidance and supervision whenever the activity requires.

Table of **Contents**

Live, Work, and

Here's a question for you, cadet: What if you won Space U's most prized scholarship—a six-week summer camp session aboard the International Space Station? You'd join a crew of real-life astronauts up there, fly around the station, conduct science experiments, eat your lunch upside down, and find out what it's like to sleep on the ceiling!

Would you jump at the chance to go?

Keep in mind that you'd be whizzing around the Earth 200 miles (354 km) above home, with no parks, swimming pools, or ice cream parlors in sight, and just a couple of astronauts for company! You'd have to go without seeing your family and friends, taking a warm shower, and eating some of your favorite foods for your entire stay. And as if *that's* not tough enough, lots of weird things would happen to your body while you were weightless— you'd get super-skinny legs and a puffy space face (see page 41), and you'd feel pretty weak when you first got back to Earth! Hmmm...does that change things?

Well, you don't have to decide now, because there isn't *really* a Space U scholarship—at least not yet. But this month, you'll get the next best thing to actually blasting off into space. We'll give you an insider's look at what life is like for the astronauts who spend months living, working, and playing on the International Space Station (known as the ISS, for short). You'll find out the answers to questions like:

■ When was the first space station put into orbit?

■ How big will the ISS be when construction is finished?

■ Can I spot the ISS from Earth?

Play in Space

- What's there to do for fun aboard the ISS?
(How do flying races sound?)

- What would it be like to play basketball
in space? What about chess or checkers?

- What's the best kind of bread for astronauts to eat?

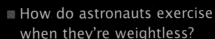

- What happens when you splash
water in space?

- What happens to astronauts' dirty clothes?

- How do astronauts exercise
when they're weightless?

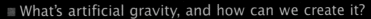

- What's artificial gravity, and how can we create it?

We'll also give you the juice on things like:

- How ISS crew members keep in touch with kids like you
- Where space station trash goes
- What happens to your body in space
- What it's like to work in a space suit
- And a whole lot more!

Space U will paint you the whole
picture of life in space—everything from getting there to
what it feels like to take those first steps back on Earth
after months of weightlessness. Then you can make up your
mind about whether *you'd* like to join a future ISS crew!

WHAT'S IN THIS MONTH'S SPACE CASE?

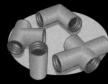

■ **Space station connectors.** Build your own space station with these handy connecting tubes. Start construction on page 11!

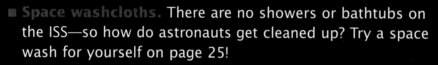

A **space travel kit,** including:

■ **Fastening tape.** These strips are great for fastening sneakers on Earth, but wait till you see how useful they are in space! Check out page 19!

■ **Space socks.** No need for shoes aboard the ISS! You can lounge around like an astronaut in your own comfy space socks! See page 19 to get suited up for the ISS!

■ **Space washcloths.** There are no showers or bathtubs on the ISS—so how do astronauts get cleaned up? Try a space wash for yourself on page 25!

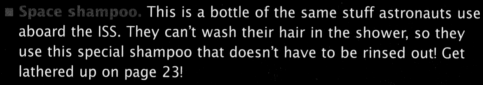

■ **Space shampoo.** This is a bottle of the same stuff astronauts use aboard the ISS. They can't wash their hair in the shower, so they use this special shampoo that doesn't have to be rinsed out! Get lathered up on page 23!

THE SPACE UNIVERSITY WEB SITE

This month you'll be able to check out real ISS astronauts at work and play on the Space U web site (www.scholastic.com/space). See them horsing around, eating space-style, and more! Plus, find out how to spot the ISS in the sky! You can also build your own space station, then watch it in action!

PLANET PASSWORD

This month's web site password is:

ALLABOARD

Complete your on-line challenges to earn this month's personalized mission patch. Then print it out, cut it out, and paste it here!

The International Space Station is a place where people can live and work in space for months at a time. It's "international" because the people who are building and using it come from countries all over the world: the United States, Russia, Canada, Japan, Belgium, Brazil, Denmark, France, Germany, Italy, the Netherlands, Norway, Spain, Sweden, Switzerland, and the United Kingdom (phew!). It's one of the biggest group projects of all time!

The first two sections of the ISS were flown into space and put together in orbit in 1998. Since then, the other parts—like additional solar panels and a robotic arm—were flown up one at a time aboard one of NASA's space shuttles or a rocket from another space agency. The ISS is still under construction, and it will take roughly forty more missions to complete, as it's currently envisioned. When it's all finished (hopefully within the next five years), it'll stretch as long as a football field and be as roomy inside as a jumbo jet!

The first crew to spend time on the ISS boarded in the year 2000 and stayed for five months. Since then, there has always been a crew of at least two people living on the space station for periods of up to six months. Turn the page to take a tour of the ISS, inside and out!

Radiators

Heat is released through these huge panels.

Trusses

These giant frames support equipment like the robotic arm, antennas, radiators, and solar panels.

Robotic Arm

The station's robotic arm moves equipment outside the station and can serve as a moving work platform for astronauts on space walks.

Space Shuttle Docking Location

The space shuttle docks here on visits to the ISS.

Destiny Lab Module

This American-made module is full of equipment for experiments and research.

Quest Airlock

On the far side of the ISS (not visible here) is the Quest Airlock. Astronauts leave and enter the ISS for space walks through this special chamber. It's called an *airlock* because it keeps the air inside the space station from escaping into space when the astronauts exit and reenter.

Unity Node

The Unity Node is the connecting passageway to the Destiny Lab, the Zarya Module, and the Quest Airlock. It also connects to the trusses and has places to hook up to modules that may be added in the future.

Soyuz

Soyuz is one of the vehicles that astronauts can ride to and from Earth. There is always one *Soyuz* spacecraft docked to the ISS at all times, in case the astronauts need to leave in an emergency.

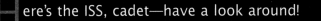

Here's the ISS, cadet—have a look around!

The spacecraft is made up of a bunch of rooms known as *modules* and smaller connecting rooms called *nodes*. The modules contain living and dining areas and laboratories for various kinds of research. Attached to the outside of the ISS are *trusses*—giant sections of framework that connect to modules, solar panels, the robotic arm, and other equipment.

Antenna

Antennas like this one let space station astronauts communicate with people on Earth.

Solar Arrays

These giant solar panels provide the space station with power. They collect the Sun's energy and use it to recharge the station's batteries.

Zarya Control Module

Zarya, which means "sunrise" in Russian, was the first module of the ISS, launched in 1998. It's used mainly for storage.

Progress Resupply Vehicle

A *Progress* Resupply Vehicle in an alternate docking location.

Pirs Docking Compartment

Pirs is one of three places where the *Progress* or the *Soyuz* can dock to the ISS. It's also an airlock for Russian space walks. Here you can see two crew members who have just entered Pirs from the *Soyuz*.

Zvezda Service Module

Zvezda, which means "star" in Russian, is the main module where astronauts live and eat. This image shows some astronauts finishing up their dessert after a meal.

Progress Resupply Vehicle

The *Progress* is an unmanned version of the *Soyuz* that brings supplies to the ISS and takes away trash.

WHAT CAME FIRST?

The ISS isn't the first space station ever built—not even close! The first one was *Salyut 1*, a Russian space station that orbited for about six months in 1971. *Salyut 2* followed in 1973, but its engines malfunctioned and it fell back to Earth after only two weeks in orbit (good thing no one was onboard!).

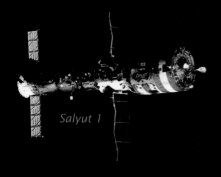

Salyut 1

The first American space station was *Skylab*, which stayed in orbit from 1973 until 1979. And the Russian *Mir* space station, which was launched in 1986, circled our planet for fifteen years!

Skylab

Mir

WHEN A SPACE STATION GROWS OLD...

Space stations have tough lives—as they orbit, they get hit by tiny bits of space junk, and they get worn down by gas molecules from Earth's upper atmosphere. They also have to deal with exposure to extreme temperatures, radiation, and the vacuum of space—all of which are bad news for the station's airlock seals and power systems. Plus, the computers onboard the station start getting more and more outdated as technology improves down on Earth.

So, rather than teach an old space station new tricks, Mission Control will bring the worn-out, empty station back down to Earth, aiming it so it drops into the ocean (though most of the station will burn up in the atmosphere before it reaches the water). This is what happened with *Mir*, and this is what will happen someday with the ISS. The ISS was designed to have a fifteen-year life span, but who knows—it could last longer!

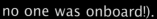

QuickBlast

Twinkle, Twinkle, Little Station

Want to catch a glimpse of the ISS? You can! The ISS is actually visible with the naked eye as it orbits over the Earth. It looks like a star moving slowly across the sky. When the station is finally complete, it will be the third brightest "star" in the sky! Where is the ISS today? Head over to the Space U web site (www.scholastic.com/space) to find out. See if it will be visible in your night sky, and then go out and try to spot it!

BUILD YOUR OWN SPACE STATION!

The ISS has grown piece by piece from its first two modules to a much bigger structure. Try "growing" your own space station to see how it's done!

Launch Objective

Design your very own space station!

Your equipment

- 6 or more empty 2-liter soda bottles (other sizes will work, too!)
- Scissors
- Tape
- Space station connectors
- Straws
- Aluminum foil

Personnel

- An Intergalactic Adult (IGA) to help with cutting modules

Mission Procedure

1 To start building your space station's first module, cut a soda bottle in half and discard the bottom portion.

2 On a second soda bottle, cut off and discard just the very bottom part, as shown here.

3 Fit the longer cut bottle inside the shorter one and tape them together. You now have a "module" with an opening on each end.

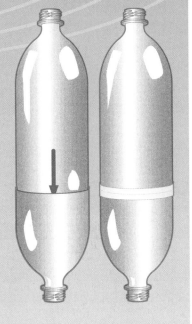

Note: Wait! Before you tape your module together, you might want to decorate it. Skip to "More from Mission Control" for ideas.

4 Repeat steps 1–3 to make a second module.

5 Choose one of your space station connectors (any shape you want!) and screw each module into one of the ends. The connectors represent the nodes of the space station.

6 Keep building and adding modules. Try using smaller bottles, too!

7 Now add solar arrays. To start, tape two straws to the side of your bottle.

8 Then cut a piece of foil and fold it in half. Tape the foil to the end of one straw. Attach another piece of foil to the end of the second straw to complete your solar array pair.

9 Add more solar arrays and any other touches you like (how about a robotic arm?). You can also try unscrewing and rearranging your modules until you find the best configuration.

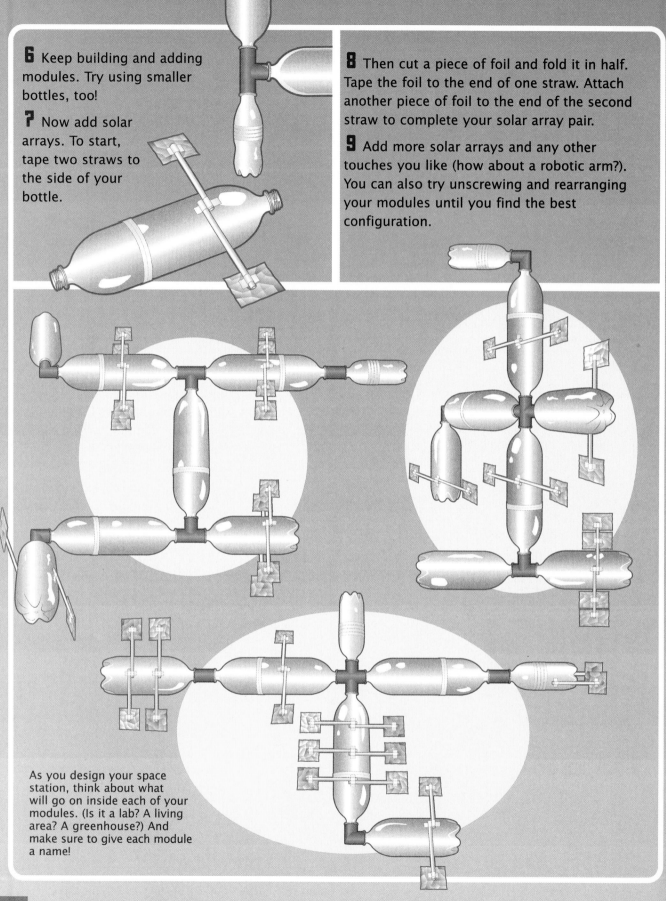

As you design your space station, think about what will go on inside each of your modules. (Is it a lab? A living area? A greenhouse?) And make sure to give each module a name!

More from Mission Control

1 Before you attach the two halves of a module together, decorate a piece of paper on one side to show the inside of the space station, with labs or living areas, astronauts floating around, or whatever else you want to have going on inside! Decorate the other side of the paper to look like the outside of a space station module. Then slide the paper into the open bottle, with the "outside" side of the paper against the sides of the bottle. Tape the paper in place before connecting the two halves of your module together.

2 Want some help decorating your space station? No problem! The Space U Department of Space Station Decoration has created lots of materials you can use to jazz up your station. They're all inside the Space Station Log pages, which you can find on this month's Space U web site (www.scholastic.com/space). The pages also include a journal where you can name your station, decide who gets to live there, and describe what goes on inside!

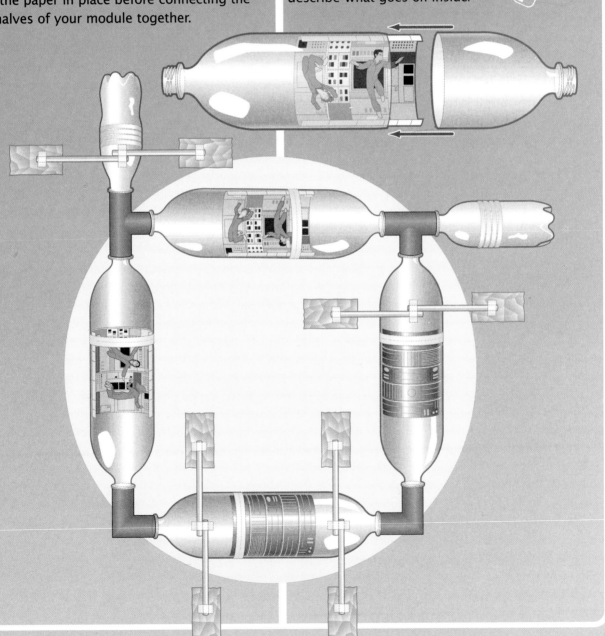

Beam Me UP!

How do astronauts get to the ISS? Well, it would be great if they could just get beamed up there, but it's not that easy. Instead, the ISS astronauts ride to and from the station on either a space shuttle or a Russian *Soyuz* spacecraft. These spacecraft also carry important supplies, equipment, and new parts needed to build the still-growing station.

The Russian spacecraft *Soyuz*

DOCK IT, DON'T ROCK IT!

Once a shuttle or a *Soyuz* craft reaches the space station, it needs a place to park! This is called "docking." Docking requires a pretty steady hand—the space shuttle or *Soyuz* pilot has to line the spacecraft up within 3 inches (7.5 cm) of the docking equipment on the space station! How would you do at docking, cadet? Try the next mission to find out!

A space shuttle docked to the ISS

WHAT'S UP? DOCK!

Mission Procedure

To practice docking, astronauts use simulators, which look exactly like the inside of a spacecraft and even shake around like one! Sound like a cool ride? It is! But until you're in astronaut school, you can practice with this method instead!

Launch Objective

▶ See if you're a dynamite docker!

Your equipment

▶ Empty soap bar box
▶ Pen or pencil
▶ Scissors
▶ Tape
▶ Two paper plates
▶ String
▶ Small paper cup

Personnel

▶ An IGA (Intergalactic Adult) to help with scissor work

Part 1: The Docking Station

1 Carefully unfold the empty soap box and lay it flat on a table.

2 On one side of the box, draw five circles in the following pattern:

3 Have your IGA help you poke through the center of each circle and cut out holes, each one large enough for a pen or pencil to fit through.

4 Close the soap box back up and tape the ends together securely.

5 On the bottom side of a paper plate, mark an "X" exactly in the center.

6 Tape the center of one end of the soap box to the "X" on the paper plate.

7 Repeat steps 5–6 for the other end of the soap box. Your docking station is ready!

Part 2: Let's Dock!

1 Unwind a piece of string. It should be long enough so that when you stand and hold one end of the string in front of you, the other end touches the floor.

2 Tie one end of the string to the top of the pen. Secure it in place with a piece of tape. Now it's time to rendezvous and dock!

3 Place your docking station on the floor with the holes facing up. Notice how it rolls around, since the plates act like wheels.

4 Standing over the docking station, hold out the string with the pen attached, and try to poke the pen through one of the holes. See how the station moves as your pen bumps into it? How long does it take you to dock? Can you do it in under twenty seconds? If so, you're a dynamite docker!

Part 3: Tough Dock

Now see how your docking skills hold up to an extra challenge!

1 Mark an "X" at the center of the bottom of your paper cup.

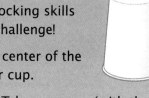

2 Take your pen (with the string attached) and gently poke a small hole through the center of this "X." The hole should be just big enough to fit the pen snugly. Make sure the pen point sticks out below the rim of the cup.

3 Now, hold out the string with the pen and the cup attached. Try docking the pen again into one of the holes. How long does it take you this time?

Science, Please!

Docking a real spacecraft takes the same kind of precision and steadiness you needed for this mission.

Here's how docking works for the space shuttle: Once the space shuttle arrives at the ISS, it has to align its docking ring with a series of hooks that are part of the ISS's docking port. The astronauts piloting the shuttle use a set of crosshairs called the stand-off cross, which looks like a giant plus sign, to align the shuttle's docking ring with the docking port. After carefully aiming for the stand-off cross, the astronauts maneuver the shuttle to meet with the docking port. When the hooks are fixed to the docking port, the shuttle has successfully docked.

Sound simple enough? Well, just like your station and docker, if the shuttle bumps into the station, it sets the station in motion, and that makes it more difficult to get the two to connect. Docking takes a lot of practice, which is why astronauts train a great deal before going on their missions. There's not a lot of room for error in space!

Docking port on the ISS

Stand-off cross

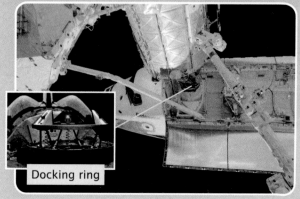

Docking ring

A space shuttle docked to the ISS

Part 2:

All Aboard!

Welcome aboard the ISS, cadet! Take your shoes off, slip on your space socks, and make yourself at home! How does it feel?

WEIGHT NO MORE!

That's right—when you're in orbit, you're in *free fall*, which means you're weightless! You can fly, float, and even flip if you want to! (To find out *why* this happens, check out *The Space Explorer's Guide to Space Travel*, where you can get the full story on the physics of free fall!)

FLASH FACT

Astronauts don't say they're "onboard the space station." They say they're "on station" for short!

I'm on station

TIME WARP!

Living on the ISS also means that you don't experience normal days and nights. That's because as the space station zips around the Earth (making a full orbit once every ninety minutes), the astronauts onboard see sixteen sunrises for every one you see!

To keep things from getting too confusing, and to stay in sync with Mission Control back home, space station astronauts stick to the same kind of schedule they'd have on Earth—except their days are quite a bit busier! How busy? Turn the page to find out!

The astronauts of Expedition 4, Expedition 5, and a visiting space shuttle are all gathered together for this group photo in the Unity Node.

NEVER A DULL MOMENT!

From the moment their morning alarm sounds at 6 a.m., the ISS astronauts have a jam-packed schedule. So what's an ordinary day onboard really like? Check out this sample schedule of a space station flight engineer:

6:00–6:10 a.m. Wake up!

6:10–6:40 a.m. Get ready for the day (brush teeth, wash up, get dressed).

6:40–7:30 a.m. BREAKFAST

7:30–8:00 a.m. Get tools and procedures together for the work day.

8:00–8:15 a.m. Have daily planning conference with Mission Control.

8:15–11:05 a.m. Conduct science experiments.

11:05–12:05 p.m. Physical exercise

12:05–12:45 p.m. Do ISS maintenance work, like moving things that have shifted around, cleaning, and replacing batteries.

12:45–1:45 p.m. LUNCH

1:55–2:15 p.m. Prepare for Public Affairs Office (PAO) event (for example, talking to kids about space).

2:15–2:35 p.m. PAO event

2:35–3:00 p.m. ISS maintenance work

3:00–4:30 p.m. Physical exercise

4:30–6:40 p.m. Have planning meeting between crew members to prepare for the next day's major tasks.

6:40–6:55 p.m. Have meeting with Mission Control to plan the next day.

6:55–7:00 p.m. Daily plan review

7:00–7:10 p.m. Prepare for TV appearance.

7:10–7:25 p.m. PAO TV appearance

7:30–8:30 p.m. DINNER

8:30–9:30 p.m. Get ready for bed.

9:30 p.m.–6:00 a.m. SLEEP

What do you notice, cadet? Not a whole lot of free time, huh? Well, astronauts *do* work very hard. But don't worry, there's some time left over for fun, too—which we'll get into a little later!

SPACE STATION STYLE

While living and working on the space station, you don't need to keep your seat belt fastened—but you may need to fasten your pencil! That's right, to keep things handy (and to stop them from floating away!), astronauts use fastening tape to make their supplies, tools, food, and other stuff stick to the walls, ceilings, floors—and even to their own bodies!

Launch Objective

> Get suited up like an ISS astronaut!

Your equipment

- **Fastening tape**
- **Scissors**
- **Sweatpants or work pants**
- **A bunch of small, important tools you use every day (like a pencil, notepad, remote control, or walkman)**
- **Space socks**

Astronaut Ed Lu shows off his space station style.

Mission Procedure

1 Find the fuzzy strips of fastening tape (not the ones with the little hooks). These are the strips that go on your pants.

2 Peel off the back and stick the fastening tape across the leg of your pants, just like the astronaut in the picture below.

3 Now cut a small piece of the prickly side of the fastening tape to stick to each of your tools.

4 Put on the pants with a shirt of your choice, and slip on your Space University space socks. You're all set to hang out aboard the ISS!

5 Attach your tools to your legs and see how well the fastening tape works! What happens as you walk around?

Science, Please!

Life aboard the space station could get hazardous with clutter floating around. A pencil drifting into an eye would not be pleasant! Plus, astronauts would waste precious time chasing after things or trying to find them. That's why they always make sure to secure their tools and supplies with fastening tape.

If any of your heavier items fell off your pants in this mission, it's because of Earth's gravity pulling them down. Since the astronauts and their tools are weightless in space, whatever they stick stays put until they remove it.

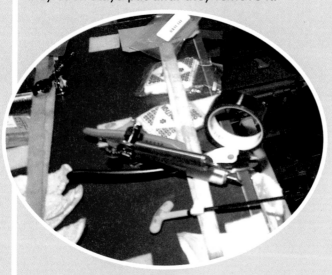

Objects can be stuck to strips of fastening tape on many surfaces inside the ISS.

As for footwear, astronauts onboard don't need to wear shoes, since they don't walk or stand on their feet. They just wear tube socks or slipper-socks to keep their feet warm.

A wrench attached with fastening tape

★Astrotales

Stick to It

Without fastening tape, things would get a little sticky for astronauts in space! So where did the big idea for the super-fastener come from, anyway?

In 1948, a Swiss man named George de Mestral noticed the way a burr (a seed pod) stuck to his dog and to his clothing after a nature hike. By examining the burr under a microscope, he saw how its small hooks attached to his dog's hair and to tiny loops in the fabric of his clothes.

Mestral worked hard to recreate the effect and finally created a sample of a hook and loop fastener. In 1955, he patented his invention under the name Velcro, which is a combination of the French words *velour* (velvet) and *crochet* (hook). Five decades later, it's hard to imagine life without the little

Ken Bowersox
ASTRONAUT

M eet Captain Ken Bowersox, a NASA astronaut who spent five months living on the ISS. He was commander of Expedition 6, which lasted from November 2002 to May 2003, and he was one of the first American astronauts ever to come home in the Russian *Soyuz* capsule.

Captain Bowersox loves to take photos of Earth from the ISS.

Question: What do you like most about living and working on the ISS?

Answer: The number one thing is being able to fly from place to place in the station. You don't just float around, you fly, and it's wonderful. The part that's satisfying about the work is that we're gaining experience that's going to someday help us leave the planet. That's a really big thing—to think about human beings someday leaving the Earth forever. That's as big as fish leaving the water and stepping up on land!

Q : What's the worst part?

A : Probably the worst part is being away from all the people you're connected with down on Earth.

Q : What new habits do you pick up in space?

A : Here on the ground people fiddle their fingers and move their legs around when they're sitting at a table. Up in space, you sort of do it with your whole body—people will do flips or they'll sit there floating and their legs will go back and forth and back and forth.

Q : When you're back on Earth, do you accidentally do anything you're used to doing in space?

A : There are things that you grow comfortable with—things like being able to take your spoon out of a can and then just release it into space, come back and get it a little later without it falling to the floor. On my way home from my very first flight, I did come close to dropping a couple things because I forgot they weren't going to float.

Q : What tools and supplies are most useful to you on the ISS?

A : Astronauts spend more time working with computers than any other tool they have. Velcro is really handy to keep things in place, and tape is useful for that purpose, too. We use common hand tools all the time for opening, closing, and putting things together.

Q : What is your favorite thing to eat on the ISS?

A : Peanut butter and jelly tortillas. Tortillas are a wonderful kind of bread to use in space because they don't make many crumbs.

Q : What did you most like to do for fun on your last visit?

A : I liked to take pictures of the Earth. On Saturday mornings I liked to eat a cinnamon roll with a bag of Russian tea and sugar, and read e-mail and news from home.

Q : Do you have a special message for our readers?

A : I hope that kids studying in school now, in twenty or thirty years, take the steps that take them to Mars or even farther!

Not Your Everyday Routine

Astronaut Frank Culbertson gets his hair cut aboard the ISS.

Everyone has a morning routine—a particular way to wash up and get dressed each day. You can probably do it while you're still half asleep, right? *The Space Explorer's Guide to Space Travel* will tell you all about teeth-brushing and using the toilet in space. But what are some *other* everyday tasks that are weird in space—especially when you're up there for months?

SNIP, SNIP!

First of all, where do you go for a haircut? Nowhere! Your best bet is to hope that someone on the crew is handy with a pair of scissors! After picking someone to be their hairstylist, astronauts hold themselves steady and use a vacuum to suck up cut hairs.

Curtain for privacy

Toilet seat (with lid down)

Foot restraint

Here's the toilet onboard the ISS. To use it, astronauts slip their feet under the bar on the floor so they don't float away. The toilet sucks waste away like a vacuum.

LAUNDRY? NO WAY!

And what do astronauts do about dirty laundry? Well, astronauts don't *do* laundry, because that would use up precious water. That's why they pick out enough clothes for the entire time they'll be on the ISS. While living on the station, they wear their clothes a lot longer than most people do on Earth—about ten days for work clothes and three days for exercise clothes.

Sound stinky? Well, that's why all astronauts are issued nose clips. Just kidding, cadet! It's not as bad as it sounds, because astronauts don't get very dirty. They stay in a controlled climate the whole time and take sponge baths every day. When an astronaut is done wearing a piece of clothing, it's put into a disposal bag and added to the other trash that gets sent back to Earth (see page 27 for more on this!).

SO LONG, RUBBER DUCKY!

Can you imagine showering with water droplets floating all around you instead of falling straight down? And imagine being near computer equipment while this was going on! Yikes! Well, that's why ISS astronauts stick to sponge baths. Even though there *was* a shower on the *Mir* space station for a while, the cosmonauts eventually trashed it (by throwing it out into space!) because it took too much time to set up and occupied precious space inside the station.

Astronaut Steven Smith washes his hair on the space shuttle with the same no-rinse shampoo used on the ISS.

Astronauts on the ISS take their sponge baths in a variety of ways. Some prefer to use wet wipes to wash their bodies. Others spray a small amount of water on a towel and clean up that way. The towels are then hung to dry, so the water can evaporate into the air and then be condensed and reused. To wash their hair, astronauts use a special no-rinse shampoo that was developed for camping and hospital use (like the kind you got in this month's Space Case!). And they leave their rubber duckies at home!

FLASH FACT

Since astronauts don't have bedrooms onboard the ISS, they pick a changing and bathing area and let the others know when they need some privacy.

QuickBlast

Lather Up!

To get an idea of what it's like to wash up in space, get out your space shampoo and wash your hair!

1 Squeeze a small amount of shampoo into your palm.

2 Rub the shampoo into your hair just like you usually do—but don't add water!

3 Now just let your hair dry on its own.

SPACE UNIVERSITY
Space Shampoo
Ready to Use
No Water Necessary
Just Apply, Lather, and Towel Dry
2 fl oz (59.1 ml)

4 That's it—you just washed your hair like an astronaut!

If your hair feels a little sticky, you can rinse it out in the shower, but for the ISS astronauts that's not really an option. Some long-haired astronauts complain that their hair feels stiff—but it's better than not washing at all!

GOOD TO THE

When you take a shower, you probably use up to 40 gallons (150 L) of water or more, depending on how long it takes you to lather up! Astronauts use only about half a gallon (less than half a liter)! See how!

Launch Objective

Wash up like an ISS astronaut!

Your equipment

▶ **The largest plastic bowl you can find**
▶ **Measuring cup**
▶ **Paper towel**
▶ **Space washcloths**

Mission Procedure

1 Place your plastic container in the sink, under the faucet.

2 Turn on the water and wash your hands for twenty seconds. If the bowl gets completely filled and starts to spill over, turn the water off.

3 Measure the water in the bowl by scooping it out with your measuring cup. How much water is in there?

4 Now wash your hands the way you would take a sponge bath in space. Fill your measuring cup with exactly one cup (200 mL) of water.

5 Fold up the paper towel and dip it into the water until it's soaked through, then squeeze as much water as you can back into the cup.

6 Use the wet towel to wash off your hands.

7 Now, check to see how much water is missing from the cup you started out with. Can you even tell that any water is missing? You saved a lot of water washing your hands that way!

Science, Please!

Water is a precious resource on the ISS, so astronauts are very careful not to waste it. In fact, most of the water on the ISS is recycled and reused. Here's how the process works: The water that is in the air condenses on cold parts of the space station's air-conditioning system. (Note: The same thing will happen if you put a cold glass of water in the bathroom while you're taking a shower—try it and see!)

LAST DROP

After the water condenses on the air-conditioning system, it's pulled off by a pump and sent through a filtering system. Then it's stored in the food preparation area, where it's heated up and used to make coffee and other drinks or to moisten dehydrated foods.

Most ISS astronauts say they don't drink the water plain, because it has a strange taste from the antibacterial treatment.

Astronaut Susan Magnus washes her hair with a towel onboard the space shuttle.

Space Washcloths

Astronauts also wash up with pre-moistened towels—like your space washcloths! Many of them find that this is the easiest way to take a sponge bath. Astronauts report that the ones from Russia are extra-deluxe: They're as big as hand towels and pleasantly scented!

Try washing up with *your* space washcloths—do you feel as clean as you do after you wash with soap and water? How does it feel different? If you were on the ISS, would you use these pre-moistened towels, or would you prefer a real towel and water?

TRASH

How'd you like it if you never had to take out the trash again? The catch is that instead you'd have to *live* with all the trash you made, keeping it in your bedroom for a whole month until someone came to collect it. Sound stinky? That's why astronauts on the ISS keep their trash to a minimum. Try this mission to see how you can do the same!

Launch Objective

> Cut down on your daily trash load!

Your equipment

▶ 2 small plastic trash bags (kitchen trash bags work fine)
▶ Marker
▶ Bathroom scale

Mission Procedure

Day 1:

1 When you get up in the morning, take a plastic bag and label it DAY 1 with your marker.

2 For the rest of the day, put *all* the trash that you make into your bag. This includes: tissues, paper towels, dental floss, paper scraps, food wrappers, uneaten food, and anything else! If you're away from home, save your trash and bring it home to add into your bag.

3 At the end of the day, tie your bag shut and place it on the bathroom scale. How much does it weigh? Now be nice and take it out with the rest of the trash!

4 Think about the trash you collected over the day. How do you think you could create less trash? Could you use cloth towels instead of paper ones? What about taking less food so you can eat it all? How about carrying your own cloth bag to the store instead of taking one of their plastic bags? See if you can think of more ideas like these!

STASH

Day 2:

1 When you get up in the morning, label your second plastic bag DAY 2.

2 Fill your bag with all the trash you make during the day, as you did for DAY 1.

3 How do you weigh in at the end of the day? Did you do better than yesterday?

4 Can you think of other ways to further reduce the amount of waste you create?

Science, Please!

Astronauts living aboard the ISS need to be careful to make as little trash as possible. Every scrap of paper or empty food wrapper has to stay onboard until an unmanned Russian spacecraft called *Progress* takes it away, which happens only once a month. So what happens in the meantime?

All of the station's trash is collected into "wet" and "dry" trash bags. The wet trash is double sealed to keep out odors. Then it all sits and waits for the *Progress* spacecraft. The trash bags and containers (including human waste) are loaded into the *Progress* cargo module, where they burn up along with the spacecraft as they reenter the Earth's atmosphere. If the trash doesn't all fit, it can also be sent back to Earth on the next visiting space shuttle.

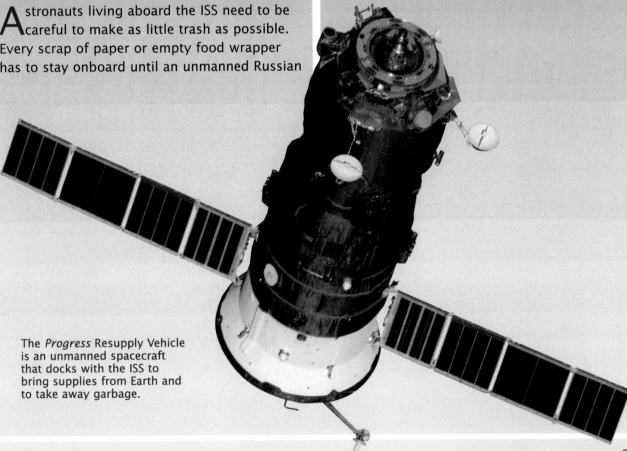

The *Progress* Resupply Vehicle is an unmanned spacecraft that docks with the ISS to bring supplies from Earth and to take away garbage.

Mission

BUBBLE TROUBLE

Astronauts need to be extra careful when they deal with anything liquid, since liquids in space don't stay in one place! But aside from the mess, drops of liquid in space are an interesting sight—try this mission to see how they *shape up*!

Launch Objective

> Make your own space-like water bubbles.

Your equipment

▶ Small glass jar or plastic bottle with a lid
▶ Water
▶ Food coloring (pick a color, any color!)
▶ Vegetable oil

Mission Procedure

1 Fill the jar a quarter of the way with water.

2 Add a drop of food coloring, screw the lid onto the jar, and shake it so that the food coloring gets mixed in.

3 Then fill up the rest of the jar with vegetable oil.

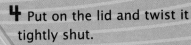

4 Put on the lid and twist it tightly shut.

5 Turn the jar upside down a few times and watch what happens!

Science, Please!

In this mission, the water drops in the oil act like liquids in space—where they form spheres (or "bubbles"). Why does that happen? It's because of a force called surface tension that makes a liquid stick to itself and form a sphere. Surface tension works the same in space as on Earth. The difference on Earth is that gravity pulls on the spheres and causes them to form raindrop shapes. In the weightlessness of space, the liquids stay in their spherical shapes, just like they do when they're suspended in oil.

Here's a water droplet floating around on the ISS. Notice its bubble-like shape!

CHEFS IN SPACE!

Years ago, astronauts had to suck their food out of tubes (imagine baby food in a toothpaste tube and you'll get the idea!). Luckily, today's ISS astronauts have a wide variety of tasty foods that are a lot like what you eat every day. And some of them are *exactly* the same! That's right, cadet—astronauts eat store-bought stuff like granola bars, peanut butter, and pudding. They also scarf down steaks, pasta, shrimp cocktail, and lots of other yummy meals, made and packaged especially for them. The food is either dehydrated or ready to eat in pouches or cans.

Space food from the 1960s came in tubes like these.

WHAT'S FOR DINNER— NEXT MONTH?

Before they take off, astronauts have to pick out what they'll be eating for the entire time they'll be on the ISS. They work with nutritionists to make sure they have balanced meals, and they taste menu samples. Then they choose an eight-day rotating meal schedule that includes American and Russian foods.

Here you can see today's space food floating on the ISS.

So what happens if the astronauts have a craving that's not on their menu? Well, since ordering a delivery would take a *really* long time, they're better off swapping meals with another crew member. Or they can turn to the snack station onboard, which is stocked with all kinds of bonus foods and powdered drinks the astronauts selected before they left.

In space, salt and pepper come in liquid form, in squeeze bottles like these. Turn to page 31 to find out why (and to make some of your own space condiments!).

PLAY WITH YOUR FOOD

When it's time for a meal, the ISS astronauts head to the Zvezda Module, where there's a fold-down table. They prepare dehydrated food by adding hot water, and sometimes they heat up ready-to-eat foods in a suitcase-sized food warmer.

After attaching their foods to the table with fastening tape, the astronauts eat their meals more or less like you would at home—with a spoon or fork.

But if someone spills or dribbles their food or drink, watch out! Instead of dropping to the floor or dribbling down their chin, the droplet or crumb will float off, and it'll have to be chased down and swallowed before it gets onto any ISS equipment! Sound like fun? It is!

This meal includes fresh tomatoes recently delivered to the ISS from Earth.

Crew members of Expedition 4 and a visiting space shuttle share a meal.

WHO GETS KITCHEN DUTY?

The ISS astronauts take turns preparing meals for each other—whoever is free at the time starts getting the food ready. But how do they decide who gets stuck doing the dishes? Easy! All the containers are just tossed in the trash, and the astronauts all wipe their eating utensils with alcohol wipes (and they're ready to use again!).

QuickBlast

Not Another Crumby Sandwich

If astronauts ever have a sandwich craving, they can always turn to an old favorite—a good old peanut butter and jelly sandwich. The only difference is that it will be on the bread of choice in space: *tortillas*. That's right! Astronauts use tortillas because they don't make many crumbs. Crumbs are a serious threat on the ISS, where they could damage equipment or fly into someone's eyes!

Try making your own ISS sandwich: Spread some peanut butter on a tortilla. Add some jelly on top if you like. Roll the sandwich up and chomp away! What do you think?

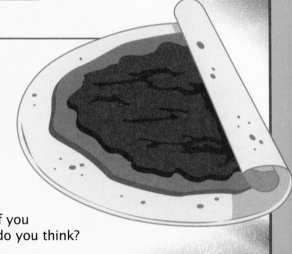

What happens when you need some pepper on your pasta in space? You can't shake it out of a shaker, since it would fly all over the module instead of straight down to your food. That's why astronauts have salt and pepper mixed with liquids—that way, they can squeeze them directly onto their meals.

Launch Objective

> Make your own space condiments!

Your equipment

- 2 paper cups
- $\frac{1}{4}$ cup (60 mL) vegetable oil
- 1 tablespoon (15 mL) ground pepper
- 2 spoons
- $\frac{1}{4}$ cup (60 mL) water
- 1 tablespoon (15 mL) salt
- Marker
- 2 plastic bags with zip closures
- 2 drinking straws
- 2 binder clips (or paper clips)
- Scissors
- Tape

Mission Procedure

1 Pour the vegetable oil and the ground pepper into one paper cup. Mix them together with a spoon.

2 Pour the water and the salt into the second cup. Mix them together with the other spoon.

3 Label the two plastic bags "salt" and "pepper" with the marker.

4 Transfer each mixture into its labeled bag and seal the bags.

5 Bend the top part of each straw down and secure it with a binder clip.

6 Pick up one of the plastic bags, tilting it slightly so that its mixture falls into one of the corners. Snip a tiny hole in the side of the bag, near the top, and slide the straw into it.

7 Fix the straw into place by applying tape across the area where the straw enters the bag.

8 Repeat steps 6 and 7 with the second bag.

9 To use your salt or pepper, hold the bag upright, remove the binder clip and gently squeeze the bag until a drop comes out. Hold the straw over the food you want to flavor, and make sure not to let the drop spill before it reaches your food!

Science, Please!

Astronauts in space often find that their sense of taste is dulled. This is probably because they have stuffy noses due to the shifting of body fluids that happens when they're weightless. This "fluid shift" means that their heads have more fluid than usual. Try eating your dinner with your nose plugged and you'll see what it's like!

Because of their dulled sense of taste, astronauts often need to squeeze extra liquid spices onto their foods to keep them from tasting bland.

Keeping all the complex machinery and systems on the ISS in working order is almost a full-time job in itself. Crew members do a lot of maintenance work, making repairs, upgrading equipment, and adding new features. Astronauts also get to perform exciting experiments, go on space walks, and do a whole lot more!

ROBOTS AND SPACE WALKS

Crew members use a huge robotic arm to help them work on the exterior of the station without having to go outside. The arm can lift and move modules and install heavy equipment. But when a robot alone can't do the job, crew members have to slip on their space suits and head outside!

Space walks are usually limited to six hours because they're so physically exhausting. Astronauts are working in pressurized suits that are stiff and hard to bend, doing important repairs and installations, while attached to the station with cables so they don't drift away.

Try the next two missions to get better acquainted with the robotic arm, and to *grasp* the challenge of working in space suit gloves!

An astronaut works in space while attached to the ISS's robotic arm.

onauts also work in the space station lab
figure out how humans can live in space
and longer. They also do studies and tests
rove the lives of humans back on Earth.
inds of experiments are we talking about?

k out this space science photo gallery!

This container brought a quail egg safely to the
ISS, allowing scientists to study the development
of bird embryos in space.

These plants were grown aboard the ISS so scientists
could learn how weightlessness affected their growth.

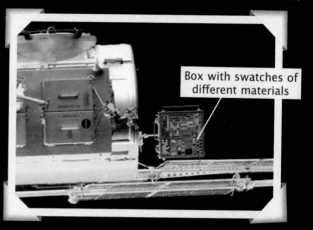

This colorful suitcase-sized box was covered in all
sorts of different materials, then attached to the
outside of the ISS in 2001. Scientists will study how
the different materials hold up in space, so they can
build better spacecraft in the future.

e science experiments sometimes involve studying
stronauts themselves! Here, Ken Bowersox (remember
from page 21?) wears a special suit that measures
s on his muscles and bones as he jogs on a treadmill.
ntists will use this information to learn more about
living in space affects the human body.

learn more? You can try experiments like
or yourself in another Space U book, *The
xplorer's Guide to Out-of-this-World Science*!

This is a close-up view of salt crystals grown on the ISS.
Crystals grown in space are larger and more perfectly
formed than those grown on Earth, where the pull of
gravity affects their structure. By growing better
crystals, scientists can make better medicines.

GET A  GR1P

Launch Objective

▶ **Get a grip with your very own end effector!**

Your equipment

▶ **2 styrofoam cups**
▶ **Marker**
▶ **Scissors**
▶ **2 regular-sized rubber bands**
▶ **Stapler**
▶ **Tape**
▶ **Toilet paper tube**
▶ **Other small, light objects to pick up (like a pencil, pen, small bottle, or toy figurine)**

Personnel

▶ **An IGA (Intergalactic Adult) to help with scissor work**

Mission Procedure

Part 1: Make Your End Effector

1 Place one cup inside the other. Draw a line around the middle of the outside cup.

2 Have an IGA help you cut through both cups at the same time along the line, and then discard the bottoms of the cups.

3 Cut a rubber band open. Fold it in half and cut the rubber band again. You should now have two pieces.

4 Repeat step 3 with the second rubber band. Now you have four pieces of rubber band (although you'll only need three).

5 Remove the inner cup and staple one end of a piece of rubber band just inside the cup, below the cut edge. Staple two other pieces at equal distances around the inside of the cup.

6 Put the inner cup back inside the outer one, making sure the rubber bands all hang out the top.

7 Tape the other ends of the rubber bands securely to the outside of the cup, so they make loops around the cut edges.

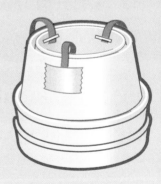

8 Holding the rim of the inner cup, rotate the outer cup until the three rubber bands cross each other.

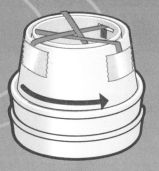

Part 2: Grab It!

Test out your end effector by picking up a toilet paper tube standing on one end.

1 Open your end effector so the rubber bands are not crossing each other.

2 Slip the end effector over the toilet paper tube.

3 Rotate the outer cup until the rubber bands grasp the tube. Pick the tube up and put it down again.

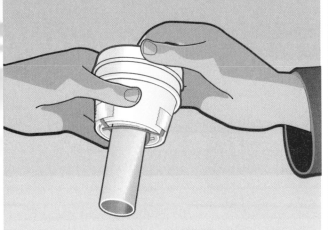

4 Stand up several light objects of different sizes in a line—things like a marker, a toy figurine, or a small bottle. Or, have a friend hold up a pencil and try to pick it up with your end effector. Can you get a grip?

Science, Please!

Now you see how the robotic arm can grab onto satellites, space station parts, and other objects while the astronauts stay safely inside the station! But what *exactly* does the end effector grab onto? The objects it grabs have a special part on them called a *grapple fixture*, which is shaped so the end effector can grab it securely.

End effector

These metal cables are like the rubber bands in your model

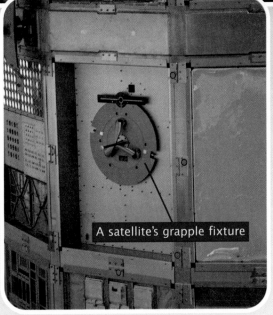

A satellite's grapple fixture

BUTTER

Did you think working with an end effector was tricky? Well, on a space walk, working with your own hands can be harder than you thought, too! That's because wearing space suit gloves makes it tough to do even the simplest of things.

Launch Objective

> Take the space glove challenge!

Your equipment

- 8 marbles
- Paper plate
- 2 empty soda bottles
- Plastic spoon
- Straight space station connector **SPACE Case**
- Timer
- Pair of thick ski gloves or dishwashing gloves
- Package of M&Ms
- Small piece of aluminum foil

Mission Procedure

Part 1: Don't Lose Your Marbles

1 Place eight marbles on the paper plate next to the two empty soda bottles, the plastic spoon, and the straight space station connector.

2 Set your timer for two minutes.

3 Now put on your gloves, which represent your space suit gloves.

4 Use the plastic spoon to put four marbles into each bottle—one by one.

5 When you're finished, screw the bottles into the space station connector. Did you finish before the timer ran out? If you think you're getting the hang of working with gloves, then move on to Part 2 for another challenge!

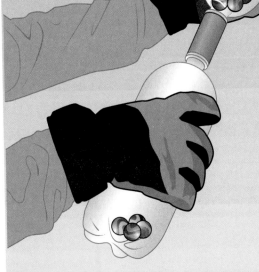

Part 2: Handy Candy

1 This time, set your timer for ninety seconds, then put on your gloves again.

2 Tear open the M&M packet and pour the M&Ms onto the paper plate.

3 Select a red M&M, a yellow M&M, and a green M&M.

4 Place the three M&Ms on the small piece of aluminum foil.

5 Wrap the foil around the M&Ms to make a small packet.

6 Slide the packet inside one of your soda bottles. Make sure the packet is small enough to fit inside, and don't let any of the M&Ms get loose!

7 After you get the packet into the bottle, dump it right back out, tear it open, and pop the M&Ms into your mouth! Could you do the whole challenge before time ran out?

Science, Please!

If you didn't finish the challenges in time, don't worry! Working with gloves isn't easy—and working with space suit gloves is even harder, because they're not only big and bulky, but they're *also* pressurized like the rest of the space suit. Space suits are pumped full of air at roughly the same amount of pressure that keeps a football inflated. Think about how hard it is to bend a fully inflated football, and you'll get the idea of what a space suit feels like!

Space suit gloves are designed so that there is little strain when your hand is resting. But when you open or close your hand, you have to push against the resistance of the glove. To feel what it's like to work with space suit gloves, try this: Close your hand so that all your fingers are pointing down. Now wrap a rubber band around the ends of your fingers. Open your hand as far as it will go, working against the resistance of the rubber band. The strain that you feel against the muscles of your hand and wrist is exactly what astronauts feel on a space walk, where they mostly work with their hands. That's why they have to practice working with the space suit gloves, exercise the muscles in their hands, and keep space walks to no longer than six hours.

Astronaut Don Pettit puts on his space suit gloves.

Curt Peternell
SPACE STATION ASTRONAUT TRAINER

In addition to all the other jobs ISS astronauts do in space, they also have to keep the space station in good working order. If something goes wrong, they have to know how to fix it! So, as part of their training at Johnson Space Center in Houston, Texas, the astronauts learn all about the space station's technical systems. Meet one of their teachers, astronaut trainer Curt Peternell.

Curt Peternell stands inside Johnson Space Center's ISS simulator, a model of the space station where astronauts train for their missions. Peternell has worked as an astronaut trainer for two years, since he graduated from college with a degree in mechanical engineering.

Question: What do you train astronauts to do?

Answer: I train them on the electrical and thermal control systems onboard the ISS. The thermal system is responsible for keeping all equipment and the temperature at a comfortable level. The electrical side covers the energy on the space station.

Q: Does every astronaut have to learn how to do *everything*?

A: Within each station crew that stays up there for three or four months, there's usually one person that's picked to be the specialist in the thermal system, one for the electrical, and another one for the computers up there. That person is in charge if communication with Mission Control is ever lost.

Q: What's the coolest part about the systems onboard?

A: It's really neat to think of the detail they've gone into to make sure that the astronauts have everything that they need. If it gets too warm up there, or if some of the equipment starts to overheat, you can't just roll down a window and air it out.

Q: What does the training involve?

A: Simulations play a big part in the astronauts' training, and there are also classes taught by trainers like me.

Q: What do you think is the hardest part of the training?

A: In my job, it's challenging to stay current on all the changes to the systems. For the astronauts, I imagine that it's hard to have to listen to people like me and soak it all in!

Q: What kind of background do you need to be a trainer?

A: The training department looks for a technical background in engineering or physics or other sciences. They also look for presentation or public speaking experience—something that shows that you can not only learn the information, which is really technical, but also explain it clearly to the astronauts.

Q: What do you like most about your job?

A: The astronauts and flight controllers I get to work with are all very down to Earth. I've been interested in space since I was in grade school, so it doesn't always feel like a job. A lot of it is learning about stuff that I want to know about anyway.

Q: Would you like to visit the ISS one day?

A: Absolutely! That would be fantastic. I'm always shooting for it.

Give Me a Break!

All work and no play would make Jack (or Al, or Yuri, or Takako) a dull astronaut! That's why, after a long week of work on the ISS, it's time to enjoy some hard-earned fun and relaxation on the weekend. Mission Control also makes sure to schedule in some free time before bed each day to give crew members a chance to wind down.

ACT YOUR SPACE AGE

Astronauts agree that the most fun thing to do on the space station is to take advantage of being weightless and just flip out—literally! They do back flips and summersaults, go for flying races, dance, and just enjoy the thrill of being afloat! And when they get tired, there's always a window nearby, where they can relax and take in the sight of the Earth below them, a view that no one ever tires of seeing or photographing. Space station astronauts can also watch movies on DVD, read newspapers and books, and play cards or other games, just like you would back home.

top: Astronaut Ellen Ochoa looks down at Earth from the window in the Destiny Lab.

above: Astronauts Ed Lu and Pedro Duque play on an electric keyboard during some free time aboard the ISS.

QuickBlast

Space Hobby

How do you think your favorite hobby would work in space? With a few changes here and there, most activities can be tweaked to work in a weightless environment. Picture yourself doing each of these four things aboard the ISS. Could you do them? How would you need to change or adapt each activity?

Check page 48 to see if your answers match what our experts at Space U came up with!

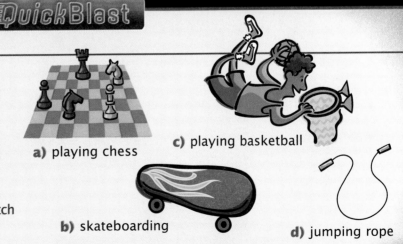

a) playing chess

c) playing basketball

b) skateboarding

d) jumping rope

Phone Home

A videoconference station in the Zvezda Module helps astronauts keep in touch with family and friends back home. (Shown here is Russian cosmonaut Yury Onufrienko.)

It can get kind of lonely cooped up in the space station for months with just a few other people. That's why Mission Control makes sure that each astronaut has a scheduled weekly videophone call to talk to friends and family. They can also talk *between* scheduled calls if they want, and they stay in touch with e-mail every day.

In addition to their friends and family, astronauts are in contact with a bunch of other people, including kids like you! Through public outreach activities, astronauts talk to school kids and answer questions about living and working in space. If you could pose a question to an astronaut onboard the ISS, what would you ask?

HAM IT UP

Another device that helps keep ISS astronauts from feeling alone is ham radio—a tool that allows astronauts to chat with people from around the world, around the clock. Ham radio is a popular term for amateur radio, a hobby for people who want to reach out to others in faraway places. The radios are a lot like powerful walkie-talkies that can reach people in other countries and even in space. ISS astronauts have used ham radio to talk to friends, family, and school kids all over the globe!

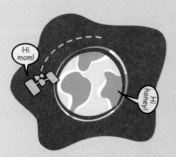

Astronaut Susan Helms talks to ham radio users on Earth with radio equipment in the Zarya Module.

Astro Exercise

Astronauts who spend long periods of time in space have changes happen to their bodies. Some of these changes are temporary, like:

- Astronauts grow taller! That's because the space between the vertebrae in their spines increases (because in weightlessness, the vertebrae aren't being pulled down, like they are on Earth).

- They get skinny "chicken legs." This is because the body fluids that normally get pulled down to their legs on Earth are now spread throughout their bodies.

- The spread-out fluids also mean that their faces become puffy and their noses get stuffed (as you learned on page 31).

Astronaut Don Pettit works out on the exercise bicycle in the Destiny Lab.

These things go back to normal when the astronauts are back on Earth. But other changes can last longer, and some could even be permanent! And we don't know for sure what happens to an astronaut's body during a stay in space of longer than six months, since so few astronauts have done it yet.

NO BONES ABOUT IT

Doctors *do* know that astronauts who spend long periods in space experience bone and muscle loss. That's because the muscles and bones that support their body weight on Earth don't get worked out in space, where they're weightless.

So what's an astronaut to do? Well, taking regular dietary supplements of vitamins and minerals helps. But the most important thing an astronaut can do is *exercise*, twice a day, *every* day! Try an out-of-this-world workout on page 43!

THE LAST STAND

Do astronauts take their workouts seriously? You bet, cadet! There's no "I'll do it tomorrow" when it comes to fitness on the ISS, because the stakes are too high. Check out how bones can weaken in space, and you'll understand why!

Launch Objective

▶ See what can happen to bones in space!

Your equipment

▶ **Toilet paper tube**
▶ **Heavy textbook**
▶ **Scissors**

Mission Procedure

1 Take the toilet paper tube and stand it on one end.

2 Balance the textbook on the tube. Can it hold the weight of the book?

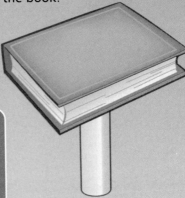

3 Now cut a small hole in the tube. To do this, pinch one side of the tube to create a small crease. Cut out a triangle from the crease to make your hole.

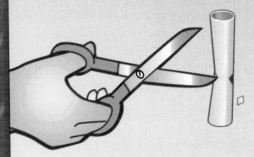

4 Reshape the toilet paper tube and stand it on one end.

5 Balance the textbook on the end of the tube.

6 Continue to make more holes in the tube, checking to see if it will still hold the book after each new hole.

7 How many holes can you add to the tube until it can no longer hold up the textbook?

Science, Please!

In this mission, the uncut toilet paper tube represents a strong, healthy bone. What makes a bone healthy? Constant reconstruction! Here on Earth, your bones are always being rebuilt, with new bone cells replacing old ones. The more you exercise, the faster your bones rebuild, giving you stronger, thicker bones.

In space, your bones don't have to support your body weight, so they don't have to exert themselves much at all. This means that, without exercise, astronauts' bones won't rebuild—they'll just gradually wear down, and the bone that withers away won't get replaced. This weakens the bone, just like you weakened your toilet paper tube by cutting holes in it. That's why it's extremely important that astronauts exercise regularly in space. Exercise puts stress on their bones so they can stand up to the stress of gravity when they get back to Earth!

OUT-OF-THIS-WORLD
WORKOUT

In a weightless environment, astronauts don't need to worry about losing weight! Instead, they work out to get their hearts pumping and to keep those muscles and bones strong.

Launch Objective

▷ See how you can strengthen your muscles with an ISS-style workout!

Your equipment

▶ **Several large rubber bands**

Mission Procedure

1 Make a rubber band chain to use for your exercises. To start, fold one rubber band around the side of another.

2 Now loop a third rubber band through the second, making the links of a chain.

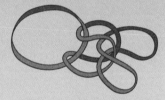

3 Continue to add rubber bands until you have a chain about 1 foot (30 cm) long.

4 Hold the chain out in front of you and gently stretch your arms open.

5 Release the stretch with a smooth motion and repeat five times.

6 Hold your arms up over your head and stretch and release again five times.

7 Experiment with making the band longer and shorter. What do you feel?

Science, Please!

Astronauts can't do floor exercises (since doing a "push-up" would mean pushing off the floor and floating to the ceiling!), and they can't lift weights (since weights would be weightless!). So, in order to get a good workout, astronauts use resistance bands that work like your rubber band chain. Keeping their arm and hand muscles in shape is important for space walks, where they need a lot of strength to work in their stiff space suits.

Astronauts also get their hearts pumping on treadmills and bicycles. How do they stay put on these machines when they're weightless? Good question! On the treadmill, astronauts wear shoulder straps to keep them in place, and on the bicycle, they wear seat belts!

FLASH FACT

When you sweat in space, it doesn't trickle down your face or body. Instead it sticks to your skin in little balls!

SO LONG!

When it's time to head home to Earth, ISS crew members hop aboard a Russian *Soyuz* spacecraft or a visiting space shuttle. Either way means a short ride of a few hours home, reentering the Earth's atmosphere, and landing. The *Soyuz* lands in the middle of Kazakhstan (a country near Russia), while the space shuttle lands in Florida or in California. But wherever it is—it's home!

RETURN TO GRAVITY

Once the astronauts hit the ground, they have to get used to feeling their weight again. They feel extremely heavy when they first land, and because their muscles aren't used to standing, they often have difficulty walking for the first few hours. They may also feel dizzy or unbalanced for a few days because the extra body fluids that went into their heads (and gave them puffy space faces!) will now head back down to their legs.

GETTING STRONGER

What's the first thing astronauts do when they get back to Earth? They reunite with their loved ones who are there waiting when they land—although the astronauts may feel too weak for a big bear hug right away! In addition to their families and friends, the astronauts often have their favorite foods waiting for them—like milkshakes, pizza, cheeseburgers, or fresh salad. But after meeting, greeting, and eating, they turn to serious physical therapy. What's involved? They do gradual workouts, starting from light to more difficult, including water exercises, massages, jogging, and lifting weights.

This astronaut just landed in Kazakhstan on a *Soyuz* spacecraft.

Part 3:
The Future of Living in Space

ARE WE THERE YET?

How would you like taking a field trip to the space station? Even better, can you imagine living there for most of your life and coming back to Earth only for vacations? Sound far-fetched? Well, for now, it might be. But scientists are working hard to make space the place for humans to live. And the existence of the space station is the first step in that direction.

CAN WE DO IT?

To live in space for long periods of time, we have to learn to work around big challenges. These include keeping people's muscles and bones healthy and strong in a weightless environment, and finding ways to deal with other health risks of space travel, like exposure to cosmic radiation. We also have to work on growing food in space so we don't have to shuttle it up from Earth, and we have to learn to recycle water even better than we do now so the space station will always have enough.

WANTED: JACK OF ALL TRADES

Ever thought of being an astronaut-doctor-dentist-mechanic-teacher-scientist when you grow up? You'd need to be in school for a *really* long time! But you'd be well qualified to live in space, where people who can fix a robotic arm and fill a cavity are very valuable. Since there are so few people up in space, there's a need for men and women who are "cross-trained" in many skills. Remember the astronauts-turned-barbers? You get the idea!

ARTIFICIAL GRAVITY

To keep astronauts from getting weak in weightlessness, scientists are working to find a way to create artificial gravity. This could happen by spinning a spacecraft—or part of it—so that the astronauts are pressed against the floor, the way we're pressed against the ground by gravity here on Earth. Try the mission on the next page to see how that could work!

Astronauts aboard this futuristic space station would be able to walk against the outer wall as the spacecraft turned like a wheel.

All Aboard!

Is space tourism really in the future? Well, it's already begun! Mark Shuttleworth, a millionaire from South Africa, was the second person to visit the ISS as a tourist, and the first African ever to fly in space. He reportedly paid the Russian Space Agency $20 million, trained for months, and even learned to speak some Russian before blasting into orbit in 2002.

Shuttleworth had NASA's blessing to fly on the ten-day mission, which was a big step forward for space tourism. NASA was not in favor of the trip of the *first* ISS tourist, American Dennis Tito, and placed several restrictions on him during his space station visit a year earlier.

In addition to hanging out in the ISS and taking photos, Shuttleworth also took some important science experiments along with him from his home country.

South African Mark Shuttleworth aboard the ISS

HOMESPUN GRAVITY

One way to deal with the problem of being weightless in space is simply to whip up some gravity! We're not kidding—you really *can* make your own simulated gravity. Give this next mission a whirl and you'll see how!

Launch Objective

> Spin your own artificial gravity!

Your equipment

▶ Paper or plastic cup
▶ Scissors
▶ 2-foot (60-cm) piece of string
▶ Water

Personnel

▶ An IGA (Intergalactic Adult) to help with scissor work

Mission Procedure

1 Have an IGA cut two holes in the cup right across from each other, near the top.

2 Thread your piece of string through one hole across to the other, and tie the ends in a knot so you have a handle for your cup.

3 Now fill the cup a quarter way with water.

4 Take your cup outside so you have plenty of room to move around. Holding the cup by its string handle, spin the cup around in circles like a windmill. As long as you're spinning the cup fast enough, the water won't ever fall out!

Science, Please!

The spinning motion holds the water in the bottom of the cup, even when it's upside down! The same idea could be used in space someday to create artificial gravity. By spinning a spacecraft at the right speed, astronauts would be pushed to the outer wall, just like your water was pushed to the bottom of the spinning cup. That means they'd be able to walk around on the outer wall like it was the ground (and feel just like they would on Earth). Sound amazing? It is!

Reach
for the ISS

So there you have it, cadet: life on the ISS. You've seen it all—working, eating, exercising, playing, and everything else about space station life. What do you think you'd like most about it? Being able to fly from room to room? Going to sleep upside down? Enjoying the view of the Earth outside your window? It's so hard to choose!

And what would be the *hardest* part of space life? Using the space toilet? Missing your friends and family? Losing strength in your muscles and bones? There definitely are some not-so-fun parts of space life, too!

As you've seen, the astronauts living on the ISS gladly take both the good and the bad. That's because they know they're part of a very special group of people who've had the chance to leave our planet and live in orbit around it. And they know that every minute they spend in space brings us closer to the day that humans can make space a permanent home!

So how about it, cadet? Will you be one of the lucky ones to live aboard a space station someday?

THE ANSWER STATION

Page 39 (**Space Hobby**):

a) A board game like chess or checkers could be played on the ISS if you attached magnets or fastening tape to all the pieces.

c) Basketball in space would mean a lot of great slam dunks! You could use a small indoor hoop that suctions to the wall and have fun! But you'd have to push the ball through the hoop, because it wouldn't fall down on its own!

b) Sorry! Skateboarding would never be safe onboard, since all the surfaces are covered with equipment and windows. But who needs wheels when you can fly?

d) To jump rope in space, you'd just have to spin the rope around your body—no jumping! If you jump in weightlessness, you never come back down!